This
be re
date

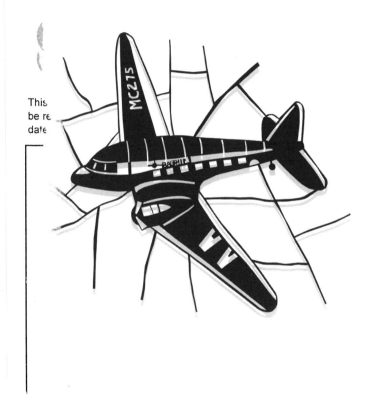

MYSTERY STORIES

JOHN TOWNSEND

SCRIBO

SCRIBO
a SALARIYA imprint

First published in Great Britain by Scribo MMXXI
Scribo, an imprint of
The Salariya Book Company
25 Marlborough Place, Brighton, BN1 1UB
www.salariya.com

ISBN 978-1-913337-61-2

Book Design by Isobel Lundie

Printed and bound in China

www.salariya.com

Artwork Credits
Illustrations: Isobel Lundie

10
MYSTERY TALES TO SEND A SHIVER THROUGH YOUR BONES...

MYSTERY STORIES

JOHN TOWNSEND

There's nothing quite like a creepy mystery to get us tingling, wondering and shivering from fears of unknown goings—on 'out there'. When no one knows the whole truth about what may be happening, things can get really spooky. Stories told of mysterious events, places and creatures have delighted and scared us in flickering firelight for thousands of years. Unsolved and unexplained tales still have great power to grip us in their scary spells. They spark our imaginations and send an icy shiver down our spines. Turn these pages and get ready to be mystified...

SOMETHING'S OUT THERE

The eyes were watching. They stared through a flurry of swirling snow that swept across the darkening hills. They blinked into the icy wind from ever-deepening shadows. As a figure moved across the field, the eyes narrowed. Bronze eyes with pin-prick cores of piercing black. Savage, hungry eyes that reflected the rising Moon.

SHIVERS

Mira was halfway across the field when she first sensed something was behind her... watching. She turned to squint through dancing snowflakes towards the frosted hedgerow. Maybe one of the farm dogs was still out and snuffling in the ditch? For there, behind a line of trees, something moved. Something big.

With her hand to her eyes, Mira tried to peer through the trees silhouetted against a pale, watery sunset. It was hard to make out the moving shadow, but she knew something was there. Something alive and staring – and she knew it had seen her. The first wave of fear rose inside her.

Was it safe to walk on across the bare ploughed field or should she turn back to the main road? But that would mean retracing her steps and passing closer to what sounded like a menacing growl. She pulled her scarf around her ears just as a branch cracked like a rifle shot. From the trees behind her, screeching rooks rose like a swarm of disturbed flies. She daren't turn back.

'Get a grip,' she told herself. 'If I cross this field I'll soon reach the track. It's only a mile then to home, where Ryan will be milking the cows. He'll get Dad's shotgun and scare "it" off.' She looked ahead but the fence and telegraph poles marking the distant safety of the road were still out of sight beyond the brow of the hill. She strode on without looking back.

Maybe the rumours were true after all? Since she'd been helping at the farm shop some evenings after school, Mira had always smiled at the daft stories from some of the staff. Just silly talk, she'd thought. The local big joke about the 'Mystery Beast'. It seemed like another of those rural myths and no more than country gossip.

Ryan said he'd seen it twice – each time from the tractor after dark. Two fierce amber eyes had stared at him before vanishing into the night, so he said. Mira accused him of living in a fantasy world like in his computer games. 'You just want to play the hero,' she told him, before adding with a grin, 'You know you're my hero big brother, so you don't have to pretend to be Superman in a tractor!'

Their cousin said he'd heard a chilling howl when he got off the school bus at dusk, just before Christmas. It came from the old quarry, and ever since, he had spoken of a werewolf stalking the woods. Then, on Christmas Eve, a woman at the local store said she'd seen a large black shape leaping a hedge in the early morning mist. It was there they found footprints in the snow. Huge prints – and the headless body of a fox. Prints that conveniently disappeared with the melting snow, before anyone thought to take a photo. Mira assumed it was all just a hoax. The young farm workers staying in the caravans nearby were always playing pranks, like making crop

MYSTERY STORIES

circles in summer to scare everyone into thinking
that there were alien spaceships landing. But
now she wasn't so sure.

Mira reached for her phone. It was a long,
lonely walk ahead in the twilight. The path
twisted over the brow of a hill and down past
the crumbling ruin of Gatby Farm. Behind her
another growl rose from the shadows. She was
now sure a large animal was somewhere among
the trees, and she was more than afraid.

Uneven ridges and furrows twisted across
the ploughed field, slowing Mira's strides. Now
she wished she'd kept to the main road where
there were lights and cars... and help. Mist was
creeping up the valley and darkness was closing
in. Her fingers fumbled over her phone as she
tried to run. An angry snarl moved closer, on the
other side of the hedge. As she staggered over
snowy ridges, her scarf loosened and flapped
away into a ditch. But she wasn't going back. Not

now, for she was at last running downhill, close to a high crumbling wall covered in ivy. Just as a faint line of telegraph poles ahead began to emerge through the mist, she stumbled and her phone dropped in a furrow. As she stooped to pick it up, a hedge just beyond the ditch shook violently and twigs snapped. Earth and stones flew as she squinted up to see a pair of savage eyes. With a terrified scream, she scrambled on all fours across the frozen mud, the dusting of snow biting at her bare fingers. Cold air rushed into her lungs and her heart threatened to burst. A thud shook the ground beside her when the creature jumped with an ear-splitting roar. Mira fell, headfirst, into an ice-filled gully.

A sudden shot ripped through the mist. The deafening crack threw a flutter of birds into the sky and echoed around the valley. Mira's ears seemed to explode as she lay panting, her hands over her head. Whimpering, shaking and with her heart pounding like never before, she opened her eyes and peered up. She dreaded what she was about to see. Nothing. Silence. She was alone in the misty field.

After lying still for what seemed forever, Mira slowly pushed herself up onto her knees and looked back across the frozen ground. Had someone shot the mysterious beast? But it wasn't a gunshot. It was the bird-scarer in the next field. It fired every half hour to keep birds off the winter crop. Perfect timing – but she knew her lucky escape might be short-lived. The creature was still there somewhere beyond the hedge, behind the wall, rustling through the trees.

Still shaking and covered in mud, Mira knew just how lucky she'd been – for she'd seen it with her own eyes. She'd glimpsed its face. For a split second she'd caught sight of its fangs and smelt its searing breath. This was no tall story to laugh about with her friends. That 'thing' was terrifyingly real and it was up to her to tell them and make them all understand. She knew it was truly horrific, and she now had no doubt that it was out there, within striking distance.

Whatever it was, just beyond the fields and prowling the woods, it was a fearsome predator. As the last light finally faded and the winter night silently closed in, the eyes still glowed through the darkness. Staring. A spine-chilling howl echoed through the trees.

By the time Mira stumbled through the front door, she could hardly talk. Her damp matted hair was caked in mud and plastered over her face. Ryan was eating at the kitchen table.

'Wow, what's up with you? Looks like you've been dragged through a hedge backwards.'

She tried to tell her story, through fitful sobs. Ryan could only listen, open-mouthed.

'I'd better get Mum,' he said. 'She's in the lambing shed with Dad and Uncle Jed. I'll go and get her while you have a hot bath. Don't worry, Mira, you're safe now.'

He didn't say any more, but he'd noticed how the farm dogs had been restless all day, as if something was on the prowl out there. Before he went outside, he fetched the shotgun they used for foxes, just in case, then headed out across the yard.

Later that evening, the police arrived. Mira was surprised at how quickly they came and how seriously they listened to her. She'd assumed they'd think she'd imagined things. But other nearby farms had recently reported sheep had been attacked in the fields. Uncle Jed lost two of his goats the night before. He said, worriedly, 'Their throats were bitten to shreds and all their blood drained. Whatever would do that?'

Possible answers to that question were given by a crime scene investigator a few days later. She arrived in a police car, introduced herself as Liz and appeared somewhat troubled. Sitting in the farm kitchen, flicking through a bundle of papers, she spoke slowly, with Mira and Ryan hanging on her every word. 'I'm afraid it's not as straightforward as we'd hoped,' she began solemnly. 'We examined fang marks in the dead goats and sheep, as well as dog-like footprints at the scene. We also extracted DNA from saliva around bite marks on the corpses. To be honest, I can only tell you what the animal out there isn't, rather than what it is. I'm afraid it's all very baffling, and a professor of zoology we contacted is just as puzzled. The crux of the matter is, we've an unknown species on our hands.'

Mira looked at Ryan. 'I may not be a professor of zoology, but I could have told anyone that. From what I glimpsed of its head and eyes, this was like no other creature I know.'

'We're certain it's not a known canine: a wolf, fox, coyote, jackal, dingo or any type of dog. One suggestion is that it might just be...' Liz paused, seeming unable to say the word. 'Some sort of Chupacabra.'

'Whatever's that?' Mira frowned, while Ryan laughed nervously.

'I've seen them in video games but they're not real, are they?'

Liz shrugged. 'Your guess is as good as mine. Apparently, a Chupacabra is a mythical beast that's supposed to kill sheep and goats. Chupacabra is Mexican for 'goat throat sucker'. Some people swear they've seen this creature in parts of America – like a large, hairless dog with big fangs and a grotesque face.'

'Sounds like a student I know at college,' Ryan smirked. No one smiled. 'In that case, let me do a search on the laptop.' He tapped the keys, gave a whistle at what he saw, and read aloud, 'Chupacabras have leathery or scaly greenish-grey skin and sharp spines or quills running down their backs. These creatures stand upright and hop in a similar fashion to kangaroos, being able to leap 6 metres in one jump. A chupacabra's face has a panther-like nose, a forked tongue and two large protruding fangs. It is said to hiss and screech when alarmed, as well as leave a strong stench behind. When it screeches, the chupacabra's eyes are said to glow an unusual red. As yet there are no reports of it attacking humans. Its victims, most often goats and sheep, are drained of all their blood, but are otherwise left intact. There is usually no other evidence of a struggle — simply two or sometimes three puncture marks in the victim's neck. Creatures resembling chupacabras have been reported in South America, the USA and recently in parts of rural Europe. None have ever been captured and no hard evidence has yet been found to prove their existence.'

Various weird images of a hideous, dog-like creature came up on the screen. Mira looked doubtful. 'I can't be sure the thing I saw is anything like that. I just don't know.'

'The alternative could be even more shocking,' Liz answered before launching into a story that stunned the family sitting around the kitchen table. 'Over 250 years ago a type of man-eating wolf was on the prowl in France, in a region called Gévaudan. Named the 'Beast of Gévaudan', it was even said by some to be a werewolf. From 1764 to 1767 it probably killed over 100 people, prowling from the forest night after night. It preyed almost entirely on women and children living in remote cottages and farms, often as they tended animals or gathered crops in open fields. No one could stop it until one heroic hunter apparently tracked it down and shot it with a special silver bullet. Some zoologists have suggested this creature was some kind of dire wolf, a species that died out after the last ice age. Maybe some have survived, but they would be very different from the modern wolf in many ways. They were much larger and stronger, and had massive skulls – fearsome predators. The wolves were once widespread, and their bones have been found in Florida, the Mississippi Valley, and the Valley of Mexico.'

Ryan snorted, 'Oh, come on – one of those isn't going to be on the loose round here, is it?'

'Just hear me out,' she went on. 'We know that biologists have been working on de-extinction projects, using the DNA from ancient bones and preserved tissue cells to bring back lost species

We don't yet know if the DNA we found here matches that of the dire wolf cloning projects going on in some countries, which are kept very secret.'

Mira sighed. 'So why would a creature from what sounds like science fiction end up here of all places?'

'A good question — and you're right, it does seem far-fetched. But we happen to know of some cloning projects being done illegally. Who's to know if one of these "resurrected creatures" has escaped or been deliberately put back into the wild? It's called rewilding. We know Australian scientists tried to clone a Tasmanian tiger. That was a predator called a thylacene that died out nearly 100 years ago. Scientists were able to extract DNA from remains and create genes. It was a large dog-like animal that hunted in Australia and had a long tail, dark stripes on its back and rump, and a pouch like a kangaroo's.

SHIVERS

Even though it's meant to be extinct, people sometimes report seeing one in the wild.'

Ryan showed a picture of a Tasmanian tiger on his screen. 'Could that be your mystery beast, Mira?'

She shook her head. 'I don't think so – but who knows? I can't be sure of anything now.' She went over to the window and peered out through the darkness.

'All I know is, there's something scary out there that could have killed me and I'll never forget its terrifying eyes and bloodcurdling growl. I just want someone to get rid of it, that's all.'

Tidying her papers, Liz glanced at Mira and said quietly, 'Judging by the evidence we've gathered, there seem to be more than one of them.'

At that moment the dogs out in the yard began to bark incessantly, with mounting alarm. Ryan went to the front door to see what had upset them.

Security lights had come on, shining across the yard and the police car dusted with snow. There were no footprints or tracks, the air was still and the cows were quiet in the barn.

'It's probably only Uncle Jed out there pottering about,' Ryan called to the dogs. 'What's got into you? Calm down.'

He returned to the kitchen where Liz was standing, gathering up her papers. 'I'm sorry I can't be more certain at this stage but we'll be investigating further, so please get in touch if you see anything more. We don't want to scare people around here so I'd like you to keep what I've said to yourselves for the moment. If not, you'll have coach-loads of monster hunters on your doorstep and the usual batch of hoaxers. Once we know exactly what creatures we're dealing with, we'll be able to take an appropriate course of action.'

'Just shoot it – or them. That's all I ask,' Mira said. 'I'm not going out there alone until then.'

SHIVERS

The dogs were still barking when they all walked outside to the car.

'You've been very helpful – and brave,' Liz told Mira, opening the car door. 'I'll be in touch again, I'm sure.'

She drove off across the yard and down the drive, the dogs still barking as the headlights disappeared from view.

Ryan was in the middle of scrambling eggs when the phone rang. He answered it cheerily with, 'Hi Uncle Jed...' His tone soon changed. 'OK, I'll come down. I'll bring the shotgun.'

He said nothing to Mira as he put on his boots and coat, grabbed the shotgun and a torch, then headed out across the yard, taking the dogs with him. He saw Uncle Jed's torchlight just ahead – and the rear red lights of the police car. Its engine was still running and the driver's door stood wide open. Uncle Jed's trembling voice cracked as he spoke just two words.

'She's gone.'

Torn papers were scattered across the drive, where drag marks led away through the snow. One of Liz's shoes lay twisted in the car, with a splash of blood on the driver's seat.

A spine-chilling howl echoed through the trees, from where eyes blinked in the shadows. Bronze eyes with pin-prick cores of piercing black. Staring... before glowing red in the dense and deepest darkness.

THE MAN ON THE
DALLAS PLANE

Nothing can really vanish into thin air, can it? Not unless it's vaporised in some way. But that just doesn't happen to solid objects in normal conditions. It certainly can't happen to people who are alive, fit and well. It's a well-known fact of science that living beings don't just change from a solid state into gas – even after a big lunch! Vanishing into thin air never happens. There again, we sometimes have to wonder...

The first time I flew in a plane was so unusual that I've never forgotten it. Although I was only 8 years old and the flight lasted less than two hours, I can still remember all the details. I can still see the man's green tie and white shirt, his jacket and shoes. The seats were blue and the air steward wore a bright red neck scarf. But it was what happened mid-flight that I shall never forget. The mystery still baffles the world more than fifty years later. Anyone who searches the man's name online will soon see what I mean.

SHIVERS

My mother and I lived in Illinois at the time and we were going to see my grandparents who lived in Texas. The flight was on a DC-3 plane from Kankakee Airport to Dallas on a bright summer's day in 1968. Although my mother told me it was a small plane, it seemed enormous to me. I suppose it held about twenty-four passengers and I remember how we were all told to fasten our seatbelts just before take-off. I was so excited as the plane began to rumble down the runway, getting faster and faster till I was pressed into my seat by the increasing speed. As we lifted off the tarmac, I looked down at the runway falling away beneath us and felt my ears pop, just as we soared into the sky.

'Wow, this is so amazing,' I said at the top of my voice. Passengers around us turned and smiled at me. I couldn't understand why they weren't as awestruck as me.

'My ears keep popping,' I added, louder than I

realised. A man and woman in the seats across the aisle looked over with even bigger smiles.

'Here, suck some candy. That always helps,' the man said, offering me a lemon bonbon.

I took it eagerly and felt it tingle on my tongue before my ears began to feel normal again.

The woman with him chatted to my mother briefly. It was one of those conversations some adults have about a child right in front of them. It was as if I wasn't there, yet they were talking about me! Why do they do that?

I was in the window seat so I spent a lot of time looking down at the hills and forests passing beneath us. There wasn't a cloud in the sky. The woman opposite looked across again and said to me, 'Look out for the mountains ahead. Below us are the woods of Missouri. We're about to fly over the Ozark Mountains where black bears and mountain lions live. It's wild country down there.'

SHIVERS

The man by the window next to her told us we were almost halfway to Dallas, when I heard him say, 'Excuse me, honey – I just need the restroom.' He stood, squeezed past her, looked at me with a smile, and headed to the rear of the plane. He wore glasses and had a greyish moustache... but that was the last anyone saw of him. I looked back out of the window as we approached the mountains. Someone said we were flying three thousand metres high. When the plane shuddered a little, my mother said it was just the wind. 'You sometimes get a spot of turbulence over mountains.'

Beyond the mountains, we saw the forests of Arkansas. The woman across the aisle was no longer taking an interest in where we were but she seemed agitated. I saw her beckon the steward. 'Would you mind checking if my husband is okay? He's been in the restroom a while and he may have got locked in.'

The steward smiled with a 'Sure' and she went to the rear of the plane. Moments later, she appeared beside us and I heard her say, 'Your husband isn't in there, madam. The restroom is empty.'

'Well where is he, then? Where else is there?'

'Nowhere, madam. He's not on the plane.'

'Of course he's on the plane. He was sitting here a few minutes ago. Please look again.'

The steward wasn't smiling anymore. She walked up and down anxiously before going into the cockpit. She emerged again with the co-pilot. They walked past us and I heard her tell him, 'A passenger is missing. A Mr Potter. He isn't there now. No one has seen him.'

I watched them go to the exit door where they touched the handle and examined the floor.

The woman opposite got up and went to join them. I heard the steward say firmly, 'Please return to your seat, madam. There's nothing that any of us can do. I'm afraid your husband has disappeared.'

'How can that be?' I asked my mother in a loud whisper. 'Is that what happens on planes?'

'Shh!'

The plane began to descend and the pilot announced we were making an unscheduled landing at another airport. We were told there was nothing to worry about, but that due to an incident on board it was necessary to land the plane immediately. Even I sensed an edge to his voice. By the time the plane landed, most of us knew they feared a passenger may have fallen from the rear door. Eventually, when we were able to leave the plane, we left through that same door and descended the steps. The missing man's wife remained seated, looking stunned. A group of important-looking men were already on the tarmac, all appearing very serious. They were speaking to the pilot in hushed voices. We only learned the details of our in-flight mystery when the story was later published in the news. One headline read: 'There one minute – gone the next'. We were amazed at what we read, but puzzled that nothing appeared to be solved.

The missing man was 54-year-old Jerrold Potter, a successful businessman. Carrie, his wife, insisted he was in good spirits on the journey. There was no reason why he should throw himself off the plane. For that was the conclusion. Jerrold Potter had opened the exit door and either fallen or jumped. But why? Nobody on the plane had seen or heard him do either. Had he mistaken the exit door for the toilet? That seemed unlikely as it had a warning on it in large letters:

DO NOT OPEN IN FLIGHT

So had he fallen against the door and pushed it open when the plane shuddered? That also seemed unlikely because the door had a heavy handle that had to be turned a full circle to release it. It would also make a noise and passengers would feel the cold air rushing in. But strangely, a chain for keeping the door securely shut was found on the floor. So what DID happen to Jerrold Potter?

Police and volunteers searched for his body over hundreds of kilometres of forests and brush, but nothing was ever found. Carrie Potter asked the search to be called off after four days because it was putting people in danger in such wild country. So she never did discover if or where he landed. When she died at the age of 81 in 1991, she still had no idea as to what really happened that day. If Jerrold Potter fell by accident, why was the door shut behind him? Was he pushed by another passenger? Did he jump deliberately? Was he in a troubled state of mind? She always denied all such suggestions.

To this day, I still keep wondering what happened to that friendly man on the Dallas plane.

As my mother told me long after we arrived in Dallas, 'It seems like it was a terrible accident. I guess we are never going to know the answer to what happened. Poor Jerrold Potter just seems to have vanished into thin air. It's one of those mysteries that's never likely to be solved. Not now. Not ever.' Over fifty years later, her words remain true.

SHIVERS

MUSEUM OF
MYSTERIES

Harrison Garcia was the joker in the pack and 'chief prankster' of sixth grade. His main aim in life was to play tricks on anyone and everyone, as well as to lecture all on most subjects. He'd yet to get the better of Miss Darovitz, but that never stopped him trying. Of course, she was always ready. Maybe she even planned her class visits to interesting places to tempt his mischief-making. Her pleasure from catching him out at his own games was obvious for all to see. Perhaps that was why she arranged the visit to the Museum of Mysteries across the city for a project on 'The Unexplained'. It would offer a chance to get the better of Harrison one more time.

'Although one of the biggest mysteries known to humankind,' she announced to the class, 'is whether Harrison Garcia will ever stop talking for even a millisecond, I would like you all to listen up so that you all know what I expect from you when we visit The Museum of Mysteries.'

Everyone sat very still, with bated breath and eagerly awaiting the arrangements. Apart from Harrison, who was about to butt in. 'I've already done some research, Miss Darovitz. They have a whole room about the Bermuda Triangle and another about mysterious disappearances – like when people just vanish and are never seen again.'

SHIVERS

'Why do you think I've arranged this outing, Harrison? I'm hoping you'll get some tips.'

Everyone nodded and laughed. 'Actually,' he went on without pausing for breath and oblivious to the stifled yawns all around him, 'there are often simple explanations as to why someone might disappear without trace. It doesn't always end in murder, you know.'

'I think the chances are quite high that it will today.' More laughs. Even Harrison had to smile, despite being disappointed not to be asked to continue his monologue.

Miss Darovitz waited for quiet before adding firmly, 'As always, I want you all to enjoy the experience but also to learn about interesting things from the displays, movies, interactive games and even the crime scene simulator. That's where you get to look for clues and to solve a murder mystery.'

Harrison was almost squealing with excitement,

waving his arm in the air and desperate to speak.

'Not now, Harrison. I have already visited the museum and arranged with the staff where the tour will begin and how we will organise you all. I'm sure many of you will be interested in the room called Cryptozoology, but I expect some of you wonder what that means."

Harrison was unable to contain himself. His hand shot up and he blurted out, 'That's creatures that we're not sure really exist because scientists don't yet have any reliable evidence.'

'Yes, a bit like a Harrison who doesn't call out. Does he really exist, I wonder? Can anyone, apart from Harrison, think of any examples of mysterious creatures?'

Although Harrison was almost jumping out of his seat in his desperation to reveal his knowledge, Ella was invited to answer. 'Unicorns, dragons and mermaids?'

Harrison took over in an instant. 'No, they're

mythical creatures. We're talking about actual beasts out there that people report seeing now and again – like Chessie, the monster like an aquatic dinosaur seen swimming in Chesapeake Bay, and the Jersey Devil or the Yeti.'

The reaction from the class was mixed. Some rolled their eyes at another of Harrison's bursts of information, while others laughed at yet another mention of his pet subjects. When it came to the Yeti, he sounded like a world expert who'd swallowed an encyclopaedia.

Ella giggled, 'Don't get him started on the Yeti – we'll be here all day!'

'Then why don't we give Harrison a challenge?' Miss Darovitz smiled. 'Is it possible to limit to just one minute what you want to tell us about the Yeti, your specialist subject?'

He started even before the stopwatch had a chance to begin. 'The Yeti, sometimes called the Abominable Snowman, is a mysterious creature often reported to live in the mountains of Asia, particularly in the Himalayas. Walking upright on two legs, it sometimes leaves tracks in snow in remote areas. Yeti actually means "ape man", as it is meant to be as big as a man and covered in black or brown hair. Over many years, local people have reported seeing a Yeti or found the remains of yaks that it may have attacked. Many expeditions have tried to find a Yeti or photograph one close-up, but so far the remote mountain regions of Russia, China and Nepal continue to hide their Yeti secrets. However, a number of zoologists believe it does exist and when I grow up, it is my ambition to lead an expedition of my own, meet a Yeti face to face and maybe even give one a high-five. Then the mystery will be over forever.'

Miss Darovitz rang a bell to show the minute was up, much to everyone's relief. 'Thank you, Harrison. Let's hope your ambition is met very soon, but now calm down before you spontaneously combust. And if you don't know what that means, just wait till we get to the Museum of Mysteries.'

'I know all about spontaneous combustion, Miss Darovitz. It's when people catch fire and all that's left is a pile of ash. I saw a documentary about it. Just imagine disappearing in a puff of smoke – but it only happens in unusual circumstances and to certain types of people.'

'Thank you, Harrison. Probably to bright little sparks who overheat from excitement. I'll bring a bucket of water to the museum, just in case of emergency.'

By the time they were lining up on the sweeping steps of the great museum, everyone had heard something about the Bermuda Triangle from Harrison's continuous commentary during their walk through the park. 'No one really knows how many ships and planes have disappeared after entering the area of sea between Florida, Barbados and Bermuda.'

After a detailed description of the dreaded 'Flight 19' when five planes and 14 men disappeared in 1945, Harrison looked very satisfied with himself as they climbed the museum steps. 'You will notice I am wearing my Bermuda shorts especially for the occasion, Miss Darovitz.'

'I just hope they don't mysteriously disappear or combust, or we're all in for a shock,' she said dryly, much to everyone's amusement. Harrison giggled, adjusted his rucksack and followed the class as they entered the foyer through impressive revolving doors. Standing under a scary banner showing a shadowy Jack the Ripper pointing to the 'Murder Mysteries' room, a grumpy-looking woman in a uniform snapped, 'Keep in line while I count you. We have to keep accurate records in case someone gets kidnapped. It often happens here.'

There were uneasy looks. Was she serious? Only Harrison was brave enough to answer their unfriendly guide.

'It's okay – I'm fully armed. My rucksack is booby-trapped.' The woman totally ignored him.

A very tall attendant behind the welcome desk smiled and winked at Miss Darovitz. No one saw her nod back at him and mouth the words, 'Yes, that's him.'

The first room everyone entered was titled:

VANISHED

'Some days I can never find this room,' the woman guide said without the hint of a smile. Harrison was the only one to laugh hysterically.

'You will find in here many true accounts, pictures and film clips about people and things that have gone missing under mysterious circumstances.'

'I know who that pilot is by the model of the plane.' Harrison was already gawping at a poster of a woman in a leather jacket. 'She's Amelia Earhart. That's an easy one.'

The tour guide gave an icy stare before launching into what sounded like an automatic response. 'Amelia Earhart, the first female pilot to fly across the Atlantic Ocean, mysteriously disappeared while flying over the Pacific Ocean in 1937. Neither she nor her Electra aircraft were ever found. You can see the full details inside that viewing booth.'

Harrison's eye had already caught sight of a huge image across the room. 'I know where that is – it's the Grand Canyon. Don't tell me that's disappeared, too!'

The guide gave a sigh before reciting her spiel, just as if someone had pressed her start button. 'Almost one hundred years ago, in the time of adventurous heroes, newly-weds Glen and Bessie Hyde planned to paddle far down the Colorado River and ride the rapids of the Grand Canyon. It was the winter of 1928, just after 22-year-old Bessie eerily told someone, "I wonder if I'll ever wear pretty shoes again." A month into their journey, the couple's homemade wooden boat was found floating in the cold canyon water. It was upright and still fully stocked with supplies. When word of their disappearance got out, newspapers around the country immediately began reporting about the honeymooners who were destined to set world records yet appeared to have vanished from the face of the Earth. One of the biggest searches in the history of the Grand Canyon failed to find a single clue as to what really happened to them, and their fate still remains a true mystery.'

Everyone stared, open-mouthed. Even Harrison was silenced, until he piped up, 'I have at least one theory. Anyway, I think it's funny that their name was Hyde. HIDE, get it?'

'Thank you, Harrison. Keep your ideas to yourself for now until you have assessed the information in detail. In fact,' Miss Darovitz whispered, to make everyone strain to hear her, 'I suggest Harrison might like to linger in this room a while to think through his theory and then give us all a little lecture to explain the unexplained. How about it, Harrison?'

'Awesome. Just leave me alone in here for five minutes and then the lecture will begin.'

'The rest of you, follow me into the Cryptozoology Room,' the guide announced. 'We can all browse for a few minutes before meeting together for a quiz. That's if the life-sized model kraken doesn't swallow a few children first.'

Everyone filed out of the room, leaving Harrison alone to explore the world of Atlantis and the *Mary Celeste*. He was over the moon. Everything had fallen into his lap. He could now execute his masterplan more easily than he'd ever imagined. Removing his rucksack with a whimper of excitement, he took out a pair of trainers and Bermuda shorts, just like those he was wearing – apart from one difference. They were badly scorched. In places they were actually singed, charred and burnt to a crisp. Next, he took from his rucksack a small vacuum flask, which he shook gently to rattle the pellets inside. Pellets of dry ice.

Harrison crept to the far end of the room where a gruesome display on spontaneous human combustion stood next to a sinister-looking Gothic archway with a black curtain drawn across it.

A notice read:

<u>DARE</u> TO STEP IN HERE AND YOU COULD VANISH WITHOUT TRACE.

He chuckled, not just because it appealed to his imagination, but because it provided the ideal place for him to hide – and to observe the horrified reactions of those he was about to trick.

Carefully placing his scorched shorts on the floor beside the burnt trainers, he unscrewed his flask and shook dry-ice pellets into each trainer and inside each pocket of the shorts. Immediately, as the temperature in the warm room began to melt the ice, a smoky mist rose from them and drifted spookily across the floor. Almost yelping with delight at the horrific illusion he'd created, he ran to the door and shouted out, 'Help, I'm combusting,' before darting back to hide behind the curtain. Within seconds, he was peeping out at the startled faces of his class, the tour guide and Miss Darovitz as they stared at the smouldering remains of Harrison Garcia beside a banner saying, 'The Mystery of Human Spontaneous Combustion'. He heard them gasp but didn't notice his teacher and the guide stifling their giggles. 'Brace yourselves for the next bit, children,' she spluttered.

The grand finale was not as Harrison expected. He felt a tap on his shoulder, turned around and screamed. He was standing face to face with an enormous Yeti. It growled, breathed down his neck with a spine-chilling snarl and bared its fearsome teeth.

Harrison burst through the curtains into the crowd still staring at his smoking remains. They turned to laugh at the approaching Yeti, now with its head removed and under its arm. A man's head grinned from the Yeti suit – the tall attendant who'd greeted them on their arrival. Still breathless from total shock and gasping from such a scary encounter with a Yeti, Harrison began to see the funny side when the man gave him a high-five.

'That's your life-time ambition achieved.

You've met your Yeti face to face and given it a high-five, just as you always hoped for,' Miss Darovitz beamed. 'And I've achieved my ambition of scaring the living daylights out of Harrison Garcia in the middle of his trickery to fool us he'd gone up in smoke. But I have to say, his hoax looks very effective. A big thank you to the museum staff for playing along with my little prank to teach him a lesson!'

'It's our pleasure,' the tour guide said, smiling for the first time. 'In fact, Harrison's smouldering remains here have given me a great idea to use his technique in a new display. If it's all right with you, Harrison, I'd like to take your photograph in front of your smoking trainers and shorts to include in a fun presentation on our website. You'll be famous!'

Harrison could only grin with delight. 'Sure, be my guest. And you can give it the title: The biggest mystery of all time is coming soon...

... THE REVENGE OF
HARRISON GARCIA!'

Enough to say, a secret plot was already hatching in his mind. It would involve a lot of cunning, invisible thread, a pin, a bag of flour and a balloon. Their purpose, as in all good mysteries, is left to your imagination – a cliff-hanger for you alone to guess!

THE GIRL ON THE PLATFORM

The railway station where I live is always busy in summer. Visitors come from miles around to swim at the beach nearby. On gloomy winter days, the station is often empty. When a sea fog rolls in and engulfs the platform, it can be one of the spookiest places I know. Some foggy nights, local people talk of ghost trains silently appearing through the haze. Shadowy figures stepping off the midnight train only to be swallowed by swirling mist are one of the urban myths in our little town by the sea.

As a student, I travel to college by train most days. Since recently breaking my ankle on the ski slope, I've sometimes needed help getting on and off the train. For some reason, our station has a wide gap between the platform edge and the train. The staff or other passengers are usually happy to lend a hand. On a late November evening, I entered the station and waved at the ticket office. 'I'm going back to college for our performing arts show tonight,' I called to the station manager.

'The train's five minutes late. I'll come and help you on, don't worry,' she replied.

I passed through onto the platform where a heavy damp fog smothered everything. Even the lights of the departure board were barely visible. In fact, none of the overhead fluorescent lights penetrated far out into the fog. I couldn't see where the track was or the line painted on the platform to show the edge. The only thing to do was find a seat and sit waiting. As I peered around me, I realised that no one else was on the platform. The station was totally deserted apart from me and a dark, dense fog. I wondered if I'd be able to see the train much before it arrived. Squinting up at the departure board, I could just make out the train was due in six minutes. I smiled at the CCTV camera just in case anyone was watching – or could even see any image at all through such a thick mist.

It was so quiet sitting there. Even the seagulls that usually squealed from the station roof were silent. Then an announcement over the speakers apologised for the train running late due to fog. I had to smile as it was usually late whatever the weather.

The next thing I knew, the seat suddenly tipped forwards and threw me sprawling onto the platform. My crutches clattered beside me, as I lay face down with a bump to my head and grazed hands. Stunned and shaken, I struggled to get up onto my knees.

A fist slammed me down again, as my wallet was wrenched from my jeans. I turned and grabbed at a foot by my hand, clinging on to the ankle as tightly as I could. A trainer kicked at my face as an angry shout rang out from somewhere above. Just as I was losing my grip and knowing the foot was about to kick me in the ribs, I heard her voice. It was very calm and quiet but also firm and with authority. 'Stop right now. Let go of that wallet and think about what you're doing. You should be ashamed of harming anyone like that.'

Instead of the kicking I was expecting, I felt the foot pull away, saw the wallet drop beside me and heard footsteps run off.

'Here, let me help you up,' she said. I couldn't

see her face as I had grit in my eyes.

'I can't see,' I panted. 'Who are you?'

'A friend. Are you hurt?'

'I'll be all right. Where are my crutches?'

'Take my arm. They're right here. Now, can you pull yourself up?'

She pulled on my arms and I flopped back onto the seat. I felt her hand brushing my face.

'Don't move,' she whispered softly. 'I've got some tissues. I'll just clean you up. Here's your wallet. No money taken. I've already called for help. I recorded it all on my phone.'

She dabbed very gently at my nosebleed and used a wet-wipe on my eyes.

'Thanks so much,' I said. 'Please don't worry about me, I'll be fine.'

'I know. But sometimes we don't always know when we most need the care of others.'

I opened my eyes to ask what she meant and was amazed to see no one was there. I was sitting alone on the platform in the fog, still holding her tissues and my wallet.

'Where are you?' I asked, looking all around.

'Just coming. It's all right, the train's been delayed a bit more. It's still another five minutes, I'm afraid.' It was one of the station staff in a fluorescent jacket. 'Are you okay? You look a bit shocked.'

'Where is she? Where's the girl who helped me? I was just attacked by someone but she came to my rescue. Where did they go?'

'No one's been through – only you. I saw a guy in trainers rushing out through the barriers but there's been no one else, I can assure you.'

'That guy tried to rob me. The girl stopped him. Didn't you see them on the CCTV screen?'

'I can play back the recording to see but in this fog it probably won't be very clear.'

A police officer in a high-viz jacket emerged through the mist. 'We've had a call that someone was being attacked. Have you seen anything? A witness reported an incident.'

I tried to explain what happened, although I wasn't really sure myself. The officer looked at me as if I was stupid. 'So you were thrown to the ground, you hit your head and you didn't see anyone but you think a girl came to your rescue and mopped your brow, is that it? My colleague is looking through the CCTV record at the minute, so we'll soon see, won't we?'

I was confused but convinced I'd described everything accurately so I asked, 'But if someone reported this to you, surely you've got their details on record?'

'The call was anonymous.'

'Can't you trace the number?'

'If necessary – but it all takes police time and it appears nothing was stolen so maybe no crime was actually committed.'

'I was assaulted!' I shouted. 'Look at my face.'

'Or you fell. Accidents do happen.'

I glanced down to look at the time but my watch wasn't there. 'They've taken my watch. It's gone.'

'Are you sure you were wearing it? My colleague's said there's nothing on the CCTV.'

I was getting angry at being doubted. Such questions might be necessary but they frustrated me. 'It wasn't a special watch, but it was still mine. So that makes this a robbery, doesn't it? And as I feel like a vulnerable victim, shouldn't you be doing something more to help?'

The officer stared at me in surprise. 'We'll look into it. I'll make a note of your details and contact you if we need any further information.' I gave my name, address and number.

At that moment the train arrived in front of us. I was pleased to be helped inside into the warm and to leave the fog behind. But I couldn't forget that mysterious girl who disappeared without trace. She was to haunt me for far longer than I'd have predicted.

On the train I looked at my phone. At least that hadn't been stolen. When a message came through with a video clip from a name I didn't recognise, I was about to delete it but something urged me to open it. Someone called Gilarna Deagun wrote: 'Hi, Hope you're OK. Here's what happened. Xx.' I was amazed to see a video lasting only a few seconds showing me sprawled on the ground, grabbing at someone's foot. The next image was my attacker's face. He was laughing into the lens, holding my wallet, then he suddenly started swearing.

Now I was even more mystified. A search for the name Gilarna Deagun revealed nothing. But at least I knew I hadn't imagined her or what happened on the station. I now had proof to show the police the next day.

SHIVERS

A police officer called at my home the following evening. She told me my case, which had now been given an official crime number, was something of a mystery as a witness had provided them with information but couldn't be traced. They'd been sent the same video clip from someone called Nadia Engeler. 'We have no idea who she might be but you'll be pleased to know we recognised the face of your attacker. He's well-known to us so we paid him a visit. He denied everything, of course. However, we found a watch in his possession.'

She took a watch from a sealed pack and held it up. My watch. 'Yes, that's definitely mine!'

'We thought so,' she smiled. 'We'll be pressing charges and getting the suspect to help us with a few other enquiries, too. As to your mystery friend, we're very grateful to her.'

A few days later I was back at the railway station waiting for another late train. When it finally arrived, the guard took my crutches and gripped my elbow to help me up onto the train. Either the step was slippery or my crutch just slid from under me and I lost my grip and fell. Trying not to hit my ankle, I reached out to stop myself nose-diving down to the track, cracking my arm on the platform edge. Someone screamed as the guard tried to grab me but missed his footing. Despite the shooting pain in my arm and a knock to the head, I was aware of hands holding my waist. They pulled me away from the scary drop down to the rails under the train. The next thing I knew, I was lying on the platform with people gathering around and the guard asking if I was okay.

'It's my arm,' I groaned, 'I think I've broken it. That's all I need.'

I was aware of someone gently placing it in a sling and whispering softly, 'You'll be fine. Just like last time. All will be well.'

SHIVERS

I tried to turn my head and look up. 'Who is it? You can't do anything for my arm here.'

Her reply sounded familiar. 'Sometimes we don't always know when we most need the care of others.'

I could just see the girl's feet and blue dress. With the light behind her, I could only squint up and make out her fair, curly hair.

'Is it Gilarna?' I asked.

'Let me help you to the ambulance,' the guard said. 'We'll need to get you checked out at hospital.'

'But where's the girl who helped me?' I asked, trying to catch a glimpse of her. 'The one in the blue dress.'

'You're lucky she caught you,' he answered. 'I don't know where she came from and where she's gone but what a relief she showed up! She certainly stopped you falling under the train.'

She was nowhere to be seen.

An X-ray at the hospital showed two breaks in my upper arm. By the time the nurses had put it in plaster and checked me over for other injuries, it was getting late. Thankfully, my ankle hadn't suffered another fracture. Even so, they decided to keep me in overnight for observation as I'd hurt my head again. 'We don't want you having any funny turns, do we?' one of the nurses said, jokingly.

That made me question myself again. Had I imagined the girl on the platform? Did concussion make me think a stranger had come to my rescue? Nothing seemed to make any sense anymore.

I awoke early the next morning. It took me a while to work out where I could be. As soon as I felt my arm, I remembered. Looking around, I saw a single white rose on my bed.

'You must have an admirer,' the nurse smiled. 'She brought it while you were asleep. We didn't want to wake you.'

'Who was she?' I asked.

'I'm not sure. We'll have her name in the book.' She went to fetch it. 'Ah, here we are. She arrived at ten o'clock. Her name's Angela Gurdinia. No address or anything but I guess you know her.'

'What did she look like?' I asked, in a bit of a daze.

'Lovely smile. Kind face. Fair curly hair.'

'In a blue dress?'

'That's right.'

The name Angela started me thinking. I didn't stop thinking, either – long after I arrived home clutching a white rose.

A few evenings later, I was back at the railway station. Once more, a sea fog rolled over the platform as I sat waiting for a delayed train. With my arm in a sling, I was looking at my phone as a train going the other way drew to a squeaky halt on the opposite platform. I glanced up briefly at the light inside spilling out into the darkness through misted windows. As the carriage closest to me began to move off, I glimpsed someone waving. She was looking directly at me, holding a single white rose. For a fleeting second I caught sight of her curly fair hair, her blue dress and the biggest smile I had ever seen.

I couldn't believe my eyes. I'd seen her face weeks before. She was the person who came to my rescue when I broke my ankle on the ski-slope. It was definitely her.

Before I could smile back, the train had gone – swallowed by the fog.

'Angela,' I whispered. 'Angela Gurdinia. Gilarna Deagun. Nadia Engeler. Of course!'

In that instant, I realised who she must be. It didn't solve the mystery but at least her names told me who she was. Maybe you'd already worked it out. That's if anagrams are your thing...

TO THE LIGHTHOUSE

Though three men dwell on Flannan Isle
To keep the lamp alight,
As we steered under the lee, we caught
No glimmer through the night.

No one will ever know the truth. Not now. The sea, wind and rocks of the Flannan Isles to the north-west of mainland Scotland hide a secret that will never be revealed.

MYSTERY STORIES

Just before Christmas in 1900, a mystery on Eilean Mòr (the biggest of the uninhabited islands) sent a shiver through the nerves of all who first heard the chilling news.

The stormy seas around northern Scotland can be treacherous, particularly in winter. Giant waves and icy gales sweep over scattered rocks and jagged crags. Any ship or fishing boat caught in a storm risks being smashed to smithereens. That's why a lighthouse was built on Eilean Mòr. Its flashing light would guide sailors away from a rocky and terrifying fate. By the end of 1899, the new lighthouse was finished and ready. It needed a crew of three men to work and stay on it; three men who were ready to live in a tower on rocky cliffs many kilometres from the mainland. Crews in passing ships were grateful to them for keeping the lamp alight in all weathers. That was until the light mysteriously stopped shining over the waves. Only one year after the lighthouse began its work, the light went out. Sailors on board a boat passing the Flannan Isles at midnight on 15th December 1900 saw no light shining in the darkness. The crew safely arrived at port and reported the lighthouse wasn't working. That message was not passed on and it took nearly two weeks before the world was to hear the news of Eilean Mòr's ill-fated lighthouse keepers.

Living in a remote lighthouse for weeks at a time with no contact with the outside world may appeal to some. But it could be tough. Trips ashore, and the occasional deliveries of supplies and mail, depended on the mood of the sea. Storms could last for days and days. Then there were the rumours: scary stories were told for centuries of these deserted islands haunted by sailors drowned in shipwrecks. Even the toughest of seafarers feared to linger around the dreaded Flannan Isles.

On the 26th December 1900, a small ship made its way through the waves to Eilean Mòr lighthouse. Captain James Harvey steered towards a landing platform jutting from the rocks. As well as supplies, he was delivering Joseph Moore, who was due to take over from one of the three men completing his shift.

'That's very strange,' Harvey grunted. 'It's not like them to be too busy to come out and welcome us ashore.' He blew the horn and fired a flare to attract the keepers' attention.

No response. Nothing.

Joseph lowered himself into a rowing boat and rowed himself up to the jetty. Already he feared something was very wrong. No flag was flying, and there were no empty boxes to collect for taking back to the ship. As he climbed the steps up to the lighthouse, he dreaded what he might find. His long walk to the top of the cliff was deathly quiet. Even the seagulls were nowhere to be heard.

When he reached the lighthouse door, Joseph gingerly pushed it open. He saw only one yellow oilskin coat hanging in the entrance hall. The other two were missing. In the hollow silence, he crept into the empty kitchen where nothing stirred. Even the kitchen clock on the wall had stopped. No fire burned in the grate. It was creepily cold and still. Pausing to listen for any sounds from above, Joseph slowly began climbing the lighthouse stairs. Round and round. 'Is anyone there?'

Up and up. 'Where are you? James? Donald? Thomas?' Deathly silence.

Completely stunned, Joseph searched every room but found no one. He ran back to the rowing boat, grabbed the oars and rowed to the waiting ship to break the news. 'No one's there. They've gone. Vanished without trace. It's as silent as the grave.'

Joseph returned to the lighthouse with Captain Harvey and his crew. They searched the whole island and rocky shore. They found nothing.

Once back on his ship, the captain quickly sent a telegraph to the mainland, tapping out in Morse code: 'A dreadful accident has happened at Flannan Isles. The three keepers, Ducat, Marshall and the Occasional have disappeared from the island. On our arrival there this afternoon, no sign of life was to be seen on the island. Fired a flare but, as no response was made, managed to land Moore, who went up to the station but found no keepers there. The

SHIVERS

clock was stopped and other signs indicated that an accident must have happened about a week ago. Poor fellows must have been blown over the cliffs or drowned trying to secure a crane or something like that. Night coming on, we could not wait to make something as to their fate. I have left Moore, MacDonald and two seamen on the island to keep the light burning until you make other arrangements. Will not return to Oban until I hear from you.'

Those who received the message were horrified. After all, this was the latest modern lighthouse operated by experienced staff. What could possibly have gone wrong to lead to such a disaster?

A lighthouse logbook showed strange comments in the last entries. Thomas Marshall, who was the second assistant, had written on 12th December about 'severe winds the likes of which I have never seen before in twenty years'.

He also wrote that his boss, the 43-year-old Head
Lighthouse Keeper, called John Ducat, was in
a very quiet and sombre mood. More strangely,
the words about the 40-year-old third assistant,
Donald McArthur, were out of character. Despite
being a hardened sailor known for tough fighting
and rough living, he was recorded as being upset
and weeping. Would he really cry about a storm?
But what was really odd was that people just
across the sea on the Isle of Lewis reported no
bad weather. From 12th to 15th December, they
said conditions at sea were nothing serious. The
lighthouse wasn't hidden from view like it was in
really bad weather. So where did those 'severest
winds for twenty years' come from?

The next day's diary entry was just as puzzling.
The storm was apparently still raging and all
three men were frightened and praying for the
storm to stop. They were all used to storms, so
why would they be so afraid, secure in a new

sturdy lighthouse on a cliff 50 metres above the sea? They should have felt really safe.

There were only eight words written in the final entry on Saturday 15th December.

'Storm ended, sea calm. God is over all.' That was the night a passing ship saw no light at all at Eilean Mòr lighthouse. Something extraordinary must have struck that very day.

A search party examined the lighthouse for clues. Two discoveries puzzled everyone most. The first was the single oilskin still hanging on a peg in the hall. Why had one of the lighthouse keepers gone outside without his coat in the bitterly cold wind? And why had he gone outside at all when there were strict rules forbidding all lighthouse staff from leaving their indoor posts at the same time? It didn't make sense.

A second discovery down by the landing platform was just as puzzling. Ropes lay all over the rocks. Those ropes were usually held in a crate high above the jetty on a loading crane. Had the crate fallen off and the lighthouse keepers were gathering up the ropes when a freak wave struck and washed them out to sea? This soon became the most likely theory. That explanation went into an official report. But not everyone was convinced. Big questions remained. Would three experienced lighthouse men really be taken by surprise by a wave? The log described the sea as calm. Maybe two of the men were down on the shore securing the ropes when a freak wave struck them. The third man could have seen what happened and rushed out without his coat to save them. While wading into the sea to drag them out, was he also swept away?

Why had none of the bodies been washed ashore anywhere? Such questions remained unanswered. In fact, ever since those lighthouse keepers disappeared, rumours and stories have always been told. Lighthouse keepers at Eilean

Mòr since have reported strange voices in the wind, calling out the names of the three lost men. Sleepless nights at the infamous lighthouse were finally ended when an automatic light was installed fifty years ago. Today the building is unmanned and empty... apart, perhaps, from the ghosts.

Tales will always be told of its mystery. Do the cries of black birds over the rocks every 15th December mean the missing men were turned into crows by an ancient curse? Did skeleton pirates carry the men away to their doom? Other stories told of monsters such as a sea serpent or a giant seabird dragging the men off to be eaten alive. Maybe one of them murdered the others, threw their bodies into the sea and swam off to find a new life?

There seems no end to the unlikely theories. Some people who have seen UFOs over the Hebrides suggest alien invaders abducted the men. But however many or outrageous the explanations, one thing remains certain: we will never know what really happened all those years ago. The mystery will always remain unsolved. No more clues will be found.

The very first people to discover the deserted lighthouse must have had their own ideas, feelings and fears. Three members of the search party remained on Eilean Mòr island to ponder in eerie silence until replacement keepers arrived. Their thoughts are imagined in the last verse of a famous poem, simply called 'Flannan Isle'. It reminds the world of the Scottish mystery that still holds its shivery secrets.

We seemed to stand for an endless while,
Though still no word was said.
Three men alive on Flannan Isle,
Who thought on three men dead.

by Wilfrid Wilson Gibson (1878–1962)

THE BEAST ON THE MOOR

The moor can be a creepy place at the best of times. When the wind howls, the snow drifts into grotesque shapes or the Moon casts eerie shadows over bent and stunted trees, it's best to keep away. Anyone out alone on the bleak and craggy hilltops as dusk falls will soon see why centuries of horror and mystery have soaked into this desolate, rugged wilderness.

Little wonder that this is the ancient landscape of legends and the hunting ground of 'The Beast of the Moor'. Said to be a black panther on the prowl, the beast has been reported by shocked hikers for many years.

I had no thought of legends or beasts as I drove across country on a blustery autumn night last year. I was more concerned with arriving at the hotel in time for an evening meal and an early night. My interview the next day at the school on the edge of the moor was uppermost in my mind as my car sloshed through puddles in the darkness. When I saw a sign ahead for a layby and services, I decided to pull in for a drink and a sandwich. It was there that I saw a minibus with the name of the school on it that I was attending the next day. Its bonnet was open and a man in a tracksuit was peering inside. As I pulled up beside him, he looked up at me, his hair soaking and water dripping from his chin. He tapped on my passenger window, which I lowered to hear him speak.

SHIVERS

'I don't suppose you're heading my way, are you? I need to be back at school for a ski-trip meeting and this thing has given up on me. The spark plugs got a soaking back there.'

'Be my guest,' I said, 'Hop in.'

He sat in the passenger seat and threw a rucksack in the back. 'Thankfully I've just dropped off the last of the kids back at their home. We've been camping up on the moor in this foul weather. Last term we were up there in a heatwave. That had its moments, too.'

I told him I was hoping to get a job at his school – my first post as a geography teacher.

'I thought so, he laughed. 'You can always spot a fellow geographer! I started here a year ago. We're a good department and it's a great school for sport – but not for that old minibus. It's always packing up in remote places.'

He said his name was Kye Newton, and I guessed he was in his early twenties. 'I don't come from round here,' he went on, 'so it's taken me a while to get to know the place. The locals warn of all sorts of stuff about the moor but it's good up there for outward bound training and geography fieldwork. That's if you don't get freaked by The Beast.'

'The Beast?' I asked. 'What's that?'

'You've never heard of the Beast of the Moor? It's often appearing in the local paper – usually a fuzzy picture taken from a distance by a trembling hiker. They say it's a puma or black panther. A savage predator on the prowl for lost ramblers – or geography teachers!'

'Wherever did it come from?'

'They reckon it either escaped from a private zoo or was released into the wild by its scared owner when it turned nasty. Either way, it's meant to prey on sheep and any stray geography student. That's what I tell the kids, just to keep them on their toes.'

SHIVERS

'Have you ever seen it?' I asked, expecting him to laugh at me. Instead, from the corner of my eye, I saw his face change. He turned towards me with a look of real fear.

'What do you think caused this?' he said icily, pulling up the leg of his tracksuit. In the light from the dashboard I could clearly see deep, long scratch lines from his knee to his ankle. He rolled up his sleeve next, where his elbow was scarred with a nasty bite mark.

'You should have seen what a mess it made of my ski jacket. It was a top-of-the-range waterproof coat, too.' His voice suddenly became disturbingly serious. 'Whatever you do,' he warned, 'never go up on the moor after dark on your own. Keep away from Crag Talon Tor.'

I was about to ask him to explain everything, when we came to some traffic lights. The rain swept over the windscreen in torrents so I turned the wipers up to full speed.

'Are you staying at the Tor View Hotel?' he asked. I told him I was.

'In that case, drop me here and you can take that turning on the right. It's a good shortcut even though it's a twisty road through the woods. You'll see the hotel at the top of the hill on the left. I can soon get to school from here. Thanks for the lift.'

'You'll get soaked,' I said. 'I've got a ski jacket in the boot. You can wear that and let me have it back at school tomorrow. It's far from top-of-the-range but it'll keep you dry.'

I ran round to the boot in the teeming rain, grabbed my red ski jacket and handed it to him.

'It's a bit bright I'm afraid, but at least it's waterproof.'

He got out of the car, put on my jacket, took out his rucksack and waved as he sprinted off.

'Cheers. Thanks again for the lift. Good luck with the interview. Give them my regards.'

SHIVERS

The red jacket shone wet in the headlights before he disappeared into the darkness, as I drove off up the road towards the moor. The rain lashed across the bonnet as the car climbed the winding road through towering woods where branches swayed high above. Twigs and leaves flew at the windscreen, tangling in the wipers slapping across the glass at full speed. I squinted out at the wet road ahead, where the headlights swept across puddles churning in the wind. Just as I turned another bend, in the headlights I saw a black shape dart out of the undergrowth right in front of me. I slammed my foot on the brake, skidded and felt a sickening thud. Whatever I'd hit didn't run off, so I dreaded what I'd find when I stepped out of the car. I feared I'd hurt someone's pet Labrador or maybe a wild deer. As the rain beat against my face and the treetops swirled overhead in the wind, I looked down to see in the headlights what lay in the road.

Whatever it was, the animal lay very still, with the occasional flick of a long tail that splashed in and out of a puddle. I could see the body was moving up and down with fast, shallow breathing. The head was stretched under the dented front bumper, so I couldn't see what type of animal it was. It looked far too big to be a dog and the legs much too long. The feet were nothing like a deer's and, as I bent lower to get a clearer view, its head shot up with a snarl. I stepped back in shock as it spat and hissed before staggering to its feet with an ear-splitting roar. Lurching in the headlights from one side of the car to the other, dragging its back legs, the creature lashed out at the bumper and clawed at a headlight. With a final snarl, baring its teeth, with ears back and eyes glowering, it slunk to the side of the road, scrambled up a bank, jumped a wall and disappeared into the woods.

I could only stand there, staring in the rain.

SHIVERS

I had no doubt I had just met a fully grown panther right there in the middle of the road.

Still shaken, I got back in the car and drove the next few kilometres to the hotel. I told the receptionist what had happened and she just smiled. 'We see and hear all sorts here about the Beast of the Moor. You'll have to mention it in the visitors' book – along with all the others.'

I arrived at school the next morning and reported to reception.

'We thought you might like a tour of the school first,' the receptionist said cheerfully. 'One of our students will be with you in a minute to be your guide. Nala is Head Girl so you'll be in good hands.'

While I waited for her to arrive, I looked at the

displays in reception. One showed photographs of all the teaching staff so I went straight to the geography teachers to see how friendly they looked. At least I knew one of them already – but when I looked along the row, I was surprised to see Kye wasn't there. Instead, there was an empty space.

'Hi, I'm Nala. Shall I show you around?'

I turned round to see a beaming smile and a Head Girl badge. 'Thanks,' I said, 'Er, just one thing – where's Mr Newton's photograph?'

The smile suddenly vanished and Nala looked past me through the window. 'He was my form teacher and my favourite geography teacher ever. It was my idea to name the minibus out there after him.'

I looked out across the carpark to a smart new minibus, with the words The Newton Bus printed on its side. 'When he disappeared we had a big collection and raised enough money for a new minibus. It's what he always wanted for the school, bless him.'

'Disappeared? What do you mean?' I was more confused than ever.

'We always hoped he'd show up one day but, of course, that was just wishful thinking. In the end they had to advertise his job and I guess that's why you're here. They'll be tough shoes to fill. Or should I say ski boots? He was such a great ski teacher, too. I really miss him.'

Her eyes welled up and I could see how genuinely upset she was.

'But tell me,' I asked, unable to make sense of what was being said, 'what exactly happened to Mr Newton?'

'It was in all the papers – didn't you see it on the news? Last term he took some of Year 9 camping up on the moor. Afterwards, he drove them all home in the minibus before going back up to Crag Talon Tor in the dark. Apparently he'd left his ski jacket up there – his famously cool, super-expensive, waterproof one. They never found him – or the jacket. They found the old minibus broken down in the Tor layby. It still upsets me to think about it.'

A tear spilled down Nala's cheek before she paused thoughtfully and continued, 'They searched everywhere. Police dogs, helicopters, drones, half the school – everyone. Not a sign of Mr Newton anywhere. Eventually they had to call off the search party and fear the worst. He's not the first to come to a tragic end up there. Maybe he fell somewhere or got lost and injured or...' Somehow I knew what was coming next. She looked straight into my eyes. 'Do you think there really is such a thing as The Beast of the Moor? That's what kids here think happened. They say it got him. Do you think that's possible?'

The image of the creature I'd seen the night before flashed in front of my eyes. 'I think it might be,' I said. "I believe there really could be something out there.'

She wiped her face and tried to smile. 'Some of us go up to the Tor layby now and again to think of him and put flowers there. We built a little shrine of rocks. It's the least we can do. You'd have liked him. What a shame you never met.'

I tried to answer. Words stuck in my throat. What could I say?

'You look a bit nervous,' she smiled. 'Come on, I'd better take you on my guided tour.'

For the rest of that day I was in a daze. Nothing made sense about the man I'd met and driven in my car the day before. As soon as the interviews were over, I needed to clear my head and get some fresh air. I drove up onto the moor, right up to the layby below Crag Talon Tor. The ragged pillar of rock stretched up into a heavy sky, dark and menacing above the heather stirring in the blustery wind. I looked down at a neat pile of stones and rocks, with a small bunch of yellow chrysanthemums wedged into a crevice. A laminated label read: 'We so miss you, sir.'

My phone rang and I turned away to shelter from the wind. I should have been pleased at the phone message. The school was offering me the job. But I couldn't answer. I was totally speechless when I looked down at a slab of rock at my feet. Neatly folded and carefully weighted down with a boulder was my red ski jacket. It was definitely mine, as I felt in the pocket and found a ticket to a concert I'd been to the week before. But that wasn't all. The right sleeve was badly torn and scratched... just as if it had been ripped by savage claws. And I'm sure I wasn't mistaken in thinking that the footprints in the mud beside me were left by none other than a large cat-like beast. For the first time that day I felt certain about something.

Even so, it's only now – many months later – that I've felt able to tell the full story. After all, how can one ever try to explain the utterly inexplicable?

Shock at the Loch

As teachers go, Mrs Milligan was fairly relaxed. Particularly when it came to monsters.

'I've taught a few wee monsters over the years,' she quipped to her Year 6 as they lined up outside Nessieland, 'so I hardly think I'll be fazed by a prehistoric beastie having a paddle in Loch Ness on a summer's afternoon.' But that was before the mist came down.

SHIVERS

'After we've had a look inside Nessieland, we can go down to the loch and maybe try sketching what we see or take some photographs to illustrate our reports when we get back to school.'

'What sort of lock? A door lock or a padlock?'

'Macey Williams, you know very well that a loch is a Scottish lake. In fact, I've already told you that Loch Ness holds more water than all the lakes of England and Wales put together.'

Someone at the back piped up, 'That's the amount all the people on Earth pee in one year.'

'Too much information,' Mrs Milligan called. 'In fact, let's see if Tomas Nowak can read us that notice by the steps.'

Tomas squinted up, closed one eye and read aloud, 'A monster adventure on the shores of Loch Ness. Fascinating fact: Loch Ness is 36 kilometres long, 1.6 kilometres wide and 240 metres deep. Wow – you could hide a hundred dinosaurs in there with room to spare!'

'The thing that makes the loch so eerie,' Mrs Milligan said in her spookiest voice, 'is the water is so dark from all the peat that washes into it. That's ideal for hiding secrets, eh? And the chilly water is 6 degrees Celsius all year round. The loch doesn't freeze over even in the depths of winter. On the coldest days, steam rises from the surface of the water. That' s because it's warmer than the air. So the loch is ideal for hiding a wallowing monster – especially one that eats Year 6 children who don't do as they're told on daytrips.'

A man in a kilt and with a big bushy beard leapt onto the steps and bellowed theatrically. 'Ladies and gentlemen, boys and girls – and all little monsters. I'm here to warn you about the Loch Ness Monster, often known as Nessie. Gather round and discover more.'

He beckoned all to join him and continued his performance. 'The first record of Nessie comes from almost 1,500 years ago... when I was but a wee laddie! The year was actually 565 when Nessie poked her head up from the deep, dark waters of the loch. A man having a nice swim was promptly devoured in front of astonished onlookers. A monk, Saint Columba, happened to be passing and he commanded the water-beastie to return to the depths of the loch – which she did.' His pause was filled with laughter, cheers and boos from his listeners. Waving his arms for silence, he went on dramatically. 'Over the following centuries, many strange events have been witnessed on these shores. Rumours spread far and wide of shape-shifting water spirits dwelling below the loch. People spoke of a shy monster emerging only when mist shrouded the shores and hid it from view. But let us fast forward to the age of the camera, and a time when Nessie was forced to stir once more. In the 1930s, a road was built along the north shore of the loch. Drilling and blasting disturbed the creature so much that it burst up from the deep once more.' On the word 'burst' he flung out his arms, leapt in the air and shouted at full volume – sending a wave of squeals and giggles rippling through the crowd.

'Around this time, there were many sightings, but then came the famous 1934 photograph taken by a London surgeon. R. K. Wilson's wee snap seemed to show a slender head and neck rising above the surface of the water. Nessie hit the headlines and became world famous. The loch has been teeming with visitors ever since and we're all extremely happy to take your money in the gift shop. I also accept tips for my thrilling talk.'

Everyone clapped and cheered, before falling silent to hear him whisper in a more sinister tone. 'Fifty or so years ago, the Loch Ness Investigation Bureau ran a thorough ten-year survey – recording an average of 20 sightings of Nessie each year. Mini-submarines explored the deepest corners of the loch, observing all manner of moving shapes in the darkness. In the 1970s, underwater photographs showed what looked like a huge flipper flapping just below the surface.'

Macey couldn't stop herself calling out her burning question. 'Have you ever seen it?'

'Och aye, of course. Every morning when I feed her haggis for breakfast. Now, I'm off for my porridge while you spend a fortune in the gift shop. And, should you dare to walk by the loch, beware. If you don't meet Nessie, you'll meet the weather. We have only two types of weather here. It's either Scotch mist and raining, or it's just about to rain with Scotch mist!'

He winked, turned and strode indoors with a flourish, to the hearty applause of the crowd.

'And just remember,' he called from the door,

'if you don't believe in the monster, I'll be out of a job – and we wouldn't want that, would we?' The response was just what he wanted.

Within minutes, Mrs Milligan was trying to round up her class outside the gift shop, each child keen to show her their purchases: Nessie key rings, Nessie puppets, Nessie bath toys, Nessie pencils, Nessie cuddly toys and Nessie T-shirts showing a cheery Nessie with a speech bubble, saying 'I don't believe in you, either!'

'OK all of you, get into a smart line and we'll head off to the loch for a stroll by the water. Keep together, don't straggle and form a neat crocodile all the way.' Before Mrs Milligan could lead off, Tomas shot up his hand. 'Maybe that's what Nessie is, a crocodile?'

No one thought that was likely in such cold water so Tomas had to rethink his theory. Someone thought Nessie could be a plesiosaur and then had to explain it was a prehistoric reptile but not technically a dinosaur. As a plesiosaur could reach 13 metres long with its stretchy neck, everyone thought that was more likely — even though Tomas pointed out that plesiosaurs died out millions of years ago.

Macey shrugged, 'So what? This one didn't. Nessie the Plessie.'

The angry sky and menacing loch didn't appear promising as they stood at the water's edge.

'We'd better get sketching before the mist thickens,' Mrs Milligan suggested. 'I'll take a few pictures on my phone to use back at school. Get your waterproofs at the ready just in case and I'll call the coach driver to come and collect us.' She took photos in all directions and then stopped to watch one of the cruise boats chugging up to a jetty to moor across the hazy water. Already the hills were lost in grey cloud that sank lower and lower and filled the valley around them.

'Aren't you scared, Miss?' Macey asked.

'Not at all Macey. You know me – never flustered, never in a flap. Relaxed is my middle name. I never see problems, I see opportunities. Now, what do you think of this nice picture of the loch. Very atmospheric, I'd say.'

Macey looked at the phone closely. 'What's that?' She pointed to a black mark in the middle of the picture. As Mrs Milligan enlarged it to look more closely, her eyes widened. 'It can't be! It looks like two humps sticking up from the water and that dark shape looks just like a head. I don't believe it!' She looked out over the water to where she'd pointed the lens. But by now, nothing was visible, not even the far shore of the loch.

The muddy-brown mist was closing in, creeping like deadly poisonous smoke, choking all colour and sliding silently over the black water. It drifted, swirled and slithered, swallowing and smothering everything in its path. Hills, trees, rocks and castle ruins were devoured in minutes as the dense cloud pressed down, suffocating the whole landscape and sucking out the light.

'I'm getting scared, Miss. It's gone all spooky and creepy.'

'Just relax, Macey. Everything's fine. It's only fog. Although we can't see anything, we're all here together by the beautifully calm and peaceful water.'

Suddenly, from somewhere nearby through the mist on the loch, there rose a rumble.

Like a steamy cauldron, the peaty loch just beyond their feet bubbled and fizzed. Its surface wrinkled and rippled as something broke the surface with a fearsome hiss. Plunging splashes churned the water into a seething, boiling commotion. Waves rolled outwards and tumbled over the shore, soaking everyone's feet, causing terrified squeals. Somewhere close by, rising from the watery depths and stirring the fog into whirling wisps, a throaty growl echoed out across the loch and thundered around the valley.

'Just relax, everyone,' Mrs Milligan said as calmly as she could, to quell the whimpers around her. 'It's only the *Jacobite Queen* cruise boat chugging past. I took a picture of it earlier before the fog came down. Its propellers make a bit of a splash, that's all. Anyway, let's stroll merrily back to Nessieland for hot drinks and biscuits until the coach arrives.'

Once back in the warm and dry, everyone else began to relax as well. Mrs Milligan cheerily approached the man with the beard who'd given the talk earlier. 'What do you think this is on my phone?'

His eyebrows raised as he stared at the photograph. 'Quite possibly you've seen her. I reckon that's Nessie – you've captured the Loch Ness Monster!'

Macey was quick to answer. 'I think we heard

her, too – but Miss said we should relax as it was only the cruise boat chugging and making waves.'

He frowned and looked at his watch. 'Not now. Not in the fog it wasn't. Boats don't sail in bad weather. They've all been moored for the past hour. No boats were out on the loch when you heard that noise.' He looked very serious, lowered his voice and added, 'The only one brave enough to venture into those dark and misty waters would be the very monster itself.'

Mrs Milligan could only gulp and stare. Apart from that, she still seemed fairly relaxed. So relaxed, she didn't stir. That's because she'd just fainted with a terrified gasp – face down in the man's porridge.

THE GHOST SHIP

I was only 12 at the time. It was my first voyage as cabin boy on the ship *Dei Gratia* in 1872. In fact, it was me who first spotted flapping sails in the distance and reported the drifting vessel to Captain Morehouse. Little did we know what we were about to find.

SHIVERS

In case you are wondering, Dei Gratia is Latin for 'by the grace of God'. She became a well-known name, all because I told the captain what I'd seen that chilly December day.

There was a fair wind and the sea was choppy, although I'd known far worse. I was still finding my sea legs and was horribly sick when we first set sail in heavy seas. I always dreaded being told to climb the main mast to deliver a message to the lookout in the crow's nest. Up there you feel the swell far worse and have to cling on tight. Our ship had two masts, so it was called a brigantine. She was built in Canada only the year before, so we were both getting used to crossing the Atlantic. We were apparently 400 miles east of the Azores, some 500 miles from the coast of Portugal. The lookout pointed over to the horizon, but I happened to glance further to my left and saw a tiny speck in the far distance.

'Have you spotted that ship over there?' I

asked. The lookout held a telescope to his eye.

'That's mighty odd,' he muttered. 'She seems to be out of sorts, if you ask me. Go tell the captain.'

Captain Morehouse was concerned and he ordered us to change course. He steered us towards the ship, keeping a close eye on her strange zigzagging through the waves.

'She's going all over the place. Whoever's at the helm must have been on the rum all night.'

The closer we got to the 'drunken ship', as the captain called her, the more alarmed he became. He called to Mr Deveau, the first mate: 'That ship is definitely adrift. There's nothing guiding her and she's at risk of keeling over if no one sets her a proper course. Lower the rowing boat and investigate. Take the second mate and the boy and tell me what you find.'

I gingerly climbed down into the boat and we rowed across to the swaying ship, drawing up alongside. John Wright, the second mate, told me she was also a brigantine, an American merchant ship, and that her name was clearly painted on her stern: *Mary Celeste*.

We all shouted our approach, but no reply came. It was strangely silent apart from the ghostly flapping of the sails.

'Ahoy there – who's on deck? We're coming aboard.' We scrambled up her port side and trod the deserted deck. With no one at the helm, the wheel spun one way then the other with every wave that struck.

The sails were partly set, with some missing and torn. Much of the rigging was dangling, swaying over the deck, with ropes hanging loosely over the sides. The main hatch cover to below deck was secure, but two other hatches were wide open, their covers left strewn beside them. I was told to stay at the helm and hold the wheel steady while the two men entered the main hatch. It was eerily quiet standing there all alone in the wind and the spray, the timbers creaking and the ropes slapping against the masts. I noticed the lifeboat was missing and the glass on the ship's compass was smashed.

Down in the hold, the men saw water sloshing around – about three feet deep. The cargo of 1,700 barrels of industrial alcohol was undisturbed. The last entry in the ship's log was nine days before, on 25th November at 8 am. Her position was given at over 400 miles from where we then were. The list of people who had been on board showed there were seven crew, as well as the American captain Benjamin Briggs, his wife Sarah, and their two-year-old daughter, Sophie. *Mary Celeste* had set sail from New York on 7th November, bound for Genoa in Italy. She had battled heavy weather for two weeks before finally reaching the Azores.

Mr Deveau said the cabins below deck were damp and the captain's possessions were scattered over his bed – but papers and his navigational instruments were missing. In the galley, everything was tidy, with a six-month supply of food and water safely stowed. There was no sign of a struggle, violence or of fire anywhere. It seemed as if everyone on board had simply abandoned ship in an orderly way and rowed off in the lifeboat. But why?

We were absolutely mystified. None of us could imagine what might have happened.

We rowed back to our own ship to report our findings to Captain Morehouse, who decided to sail *Mary Celeste* to port 800 miles away. Four of us went back on board to sail her, while the *Dei Gratia* led the way.

The weather was fairly calm for most of the voyage, although we were delayed in fog, so arrived in Gibraltar a day after Captain Morehouse. I spent ten days on that haunted ship, creaking with secrets.

When we arrived, some people thought we must have killed the crew onboard that ship so we could claim the salvage money. Although we did get paid, I swore to everyone we were guilty of no such crime. That would never happen.

In time, all kinds of other rumours were told about the *Mary Celeste*. None of them made sense. Captain Briggs had been an experienced sailor and he was used to sailing in all conditions. Stories of pirates attacking the ship were told – but nothing had been stolen and there were no signs of attack anywhere. I was convinced there had been no fighting onboard. If danger had struck, like bad weather, illness or even some kind of sea monster, why ever would everyone abandon ship, without a mention in the log and no sign of panic left behind? There seemed no reason whatsoever why all ten people would have disappeared at once, leaving a perfectly good ship and its expensive cargo to the ravages of the angry ocean. Those ten people and the lifeboat were never found. The disappearance of the *Mary Celeste* will remain one of the great mysteries of the sea. Even today, many years later, as I write this at the age of 65, I cannot forget the chilling feeling of being on that doomed ship as a boy. It's as if her shivering ghosts entered my very bones. In fact, her final fate struck just three years later when she was wrecked on a reef — sinking with all her dark secrets, to be lost forever beneath the all-knowing waves.

SHARK MURDER MYSTERY

April 1935

To The Sydney Police
Department, Australia

They say there's no such thing as
the perfect murder. That's because
murderers always leave clues behind

somewhere. Clues that can lead to an arrest. Let me tell you otherwise.

I have just committed the perfect murder. You will never find the body and never know what happened. I will walk free for the rest of my life and you'll never know who I am.

I am only telling you this to get my own back. Some of your officers think they're so clever and better than me. Well, they're so wrong.

I simply wanted to tell you I've beaten you all and that gives me the greatest pleasure. I've murdered someone who tried to blackmail me and I'm going to get away with it. Just how great is the Australian Police Force after all?

You're never going to solve this crime because I'm just too smart for you.

Yours smugly,
A Successful Murderer
(never to be arrested!)

'Welcome everyone to our fantastic new exhibit. Just a few days ago our tiger shark was swimming in the ocean, but now you can watch this great predator of the deep in a feeding frenzy right here. One of the most dangerous sharks off our coast, tiger sharks don't just have stripes like a tiger, they have tiger ferocity, too. Don't get too close – it bites!'

It was a big day out for families on the Coogee beaches near Sydney, Australia. Being Anzac Day, the public holiday held on 25th April, visitors flocked to the coast. The great new attraction at the aquarium was a deadly 5-metre-long tiger shark swimming safely behind toughened glass. Crowds watched in awe as the fearsome predator circled its tank in the build-up to feeding time. Posing glamorously above the tank behind a safety rail, two assistants held up buckets of fish. But before the dramatic countdown to dinner began, the shark suddenly thrashed around, twisting and turning, as if distressed. People gasped as it rolled over, retched and coughed up a disgusting cloud of sick. Those at the front were horrified to see what was spat out from the shark's jaws and slowly sank to the bottom of the aquarium – a human arm.

Staff quickly moved the crowds on and screened off the shark tank. A diver then had the risky job of retrieving the arm for the police to examine. It was all that remained of the poor victim of a shark attack – or so it seemed at first.

When the police arrived, they were convinced 'the shark-arm incident' was a prank – either by the staff themselves or by local medical students who'd stolen an arm from the mortuary. As no one had reported any shark attacks lately, it all seemed like a big publicity stunt. But this was not a joke. When the arm was examined properly, a rope was found tied around the wrist. More sinister was the verdict that the arm hadn't been bitten off by the shark at all. It had been cut off with a blunt knife after death. The victim, it seemed, had been murdered. Had the body been cut up and dumped at sea? Tiger sharks are well known for swallowing whole anything they find lying around in the ocean. So the shark in the aquarium had probably gulped down the arm from the seabed just hours before it was captured. Then, after one big fit of indigestion, it brought up its gruesome lunch in full view of the public's gaze.

SHIVERS

The police had a big mystery to solve. How could they find out whose arm it was? By the 1930s, the science of fingerprints was developing, so police scientists set about taking prints from the dead fingers and trying to match them against anyone on their records. Before the age of computers, this had to be done by many officers searching through thousands of paper records. Meanwhile, there was one important clue. The arm was a man's left arm, with a distinct tattoo on the shoulder of two boxers fighting. The police printed pictures of it in newspapers to see if anyone recognised it. Sure enough, Mrs Smith called to say the arm belonged to her husband who had mysteriously disappeared recently. He was 40-year-old James Smith, a former boxer and builder. The fingerprints also matched his police record, as he had previously been arrested for minor crimes. But now the police had another mystery. Who killed James Smith?

Mrs Smith told police, 'The last I saw of James was on Monday morning, the 8th of April. He was going out fishing with a friend, although he didn't say who that was. When he didn't come home that night I wasn't too concerned at first. After another day or so, I began to get worried. He was due back at work at the boatbuilding yard. One night I had a mysterious phone call from a man I didn't know. He said, "Don't worry, Jimmy will be home in three days' time." But Jimmy never made it home.'

She gave the police the names of her husband's friends and contacts. Some of them said they had seen him with a man called Patrick Brady on 8th April, at a hotel bar in Cronulla nearby. The police knew Brady had been involved in forgery and smuggling so they went to question him. Interestingly, he rented a cottage in Cronulla so they searched it for clues. Nothing – except a witness said a big trunk that was usually in a bedroom was missing. Just right for hiding a body inside and rowing it out to sea?

Patrick Brady seemed to be lying. He said he hadn't been in Cronulla on 8th April. The police arrested him, despite his angry protests. 'You can't prove anything!'

Just days later, a speedboat sped out of control in Sydney Harbour. The police gave chase and when they finally caught the driver, he turned out to be a boatbuilder called Reginal Holmes, none other than James Smith's boss. He was in a confused state, having just been attacked and shot by unknown attackers. Then came an interesting confession. A few days before, Patrick Brady had admitted to him he'd killed James Smith. It was because Smith had threatened to tell the police of Brady's crimes unless he paid up – Smith was attempting to blackmail him. The police promptly charged Brady with murder but before Holmes could testify in court, he was found shot dead. Someone had wanted him silenced. One of Brady's gang, perhaps?

So now the evidence against Patrick Brady wasn't enough to convict him for the murder of James Smith. Without modern forensic science, nothing could prove Brady was guilty of the crime. Not to be outdone, the police arrested him again for forgery, so Brady ended up in prison after all. How he must have cursed his luck – and the shark. If that tiger shark hadn't swallowed an arm, been caught and coughed it up in public, Patrick Brady would have got away with all his crimes. Who could have guessed the chances of that happening?

Even so, in the end, the official outcome of James Smith's murder remained 'unsolved'.

SHIVERS

September 1935

Dear Patrick Brady,

They say there's no such thing as the perfect murder. Correct.

So you think you've got away with murder, eh? Let's face it, prison is still prison! So it seems you're not so smart after all. Maybe, as you spend time behind bars, you might begin to realise that we're much smarter than you'll ever be. Once that shark coughed up, things began to look very fishy indeed!

With love from the Sydney Police

P.S. Warning: sharks can be 'ARMFUL to life and limb!

NEVER SAY NEVER

My great-grandma is amazing. She's nearly ninety now, but her memory is as sharp as a pin. Ever since I can remember, she's told fantastic stories. What's more, they all really happened because she was actually there when some incredible mysteries unfolded. I suppose living so long in many different places, she's happened to come across strange events. It's just as well I've recorded her tales. There's nothing quite like hearing a story from someone who was there at the time...

As a girl, I lived in Colorado. I guess you could call it the sort of town you see in Wild West cowboy movies. Most folks lived by scratching a living out of the land. We had a few cows and chickens on a small plot. Our neighbours were the Olsens, who were also farmers until they hit the jackpot. Something happened one day that changed their lives and put our town on the map. It's a mystery to me how all that happened. After all, how can anyone live without a head? Impossible as it sounds, never say never.

I sometimes went round to see Lloyd and Clara Olsen. One day in 1945, Mr Olsen (as

I called him) asked me if I'd like to see one of his roosters. I remember I just said, 'Ain't one rooster just like any other? I've seen hundreds of them.'

'Not like mine,' he chuckled. Then he said, 'Last evening Clara asked me to get a rooster for her to make chicken stew. I went up the yard with my axe and picked a good plump rooster for the chop. I swung the axe, off came its head and I waited for our supper to stop flapping. The thing is, that bird just didn't stop. I went indoors to wait and deal with it later but when I returned to collect supper, I reached down and flap flap flap! The only thing to do was to come back the next day when that headless chicken had finally stopped flapping. We went without stew that night. Next morning, that bird was still perched there, alive and headless. So, I set about giving the rooster breakfast. Well, why not? I fed it with grain crushed in milk with an eye-dropper down its neck. Now do you want to see my rooster?'

'Yes sir,' I said. 'You bet.'

Mrs Olsen showed me how she cleared the chicken's throat with a syringe when it spluttered or choked, then fed it with porridge in a dropper. She said they were calling the bird 'Miracle Mike, the Wonder Chicken', and no longer wanted to eat him in a stew but to get rich from owning a living headless chicken. Believe it or not, news of Miracle Mike travelled far beyond our town. After our local newspaper printed a story about him, it took less than a month for a man called Hope Wade to show up. He ran sideshows at fairs and he saw a way to make a quick buck by putting that chicken in a freak show. He said people would pay 10 cents to see Miracle Mike.

All this time, I kept asking everyone to explain to me the mystery of how anything could live without a head – in particular, without a brain. Was the answer a no-brainer? The Olsens were also mystified, so they took their now-famous chicken to a university in Salt Lake City where scientists made a careful study. They said the bird's brainstem, which is like a tube in its neck, was still working and that it was able to control the most important functions of a chicken's body. A freak blood clot had stopped the chicken from bleeding to death.

When the story of Miracle Mike appeared in *Life Magazine*, he became so famous that he went on tour and everyone flocked to see him. My Ma said he earned the Olsens about $4,500 per month! That was unheard of back then.

I remember being so upset when I heard the sad news. Miracle Mike was on show in Arizona when the Olsens booked into a motel in Phoenix. On the night of March 17th, 1947, they were woken by the sound of their beloved chicken choking.

'Honey, where's that syringe to unclog Mike's throat?'

SHIVERS

'I dunno, dear – it might be in my purse in the automobile. I'm sure I had it here some place.'

But it was already too late. While they tried to find something to clear Mike's airway, their famous fowl dropped from his perch and died. The show was finally over. Can you believe Mike had survived for an astonishing year and a half without a head? How we all missed him. Even today, the town remembers Miracle Mike with a metal sculpture of his headless body. They now host a Headless Chicken Carnival each year in his honour. As far as I'm concerned, all that fuss, as well as a creature surviving so long without a head, is one of those great mysteries. Just like Mike, I'll never get my head around it!

When I grew up and married, we moved north west to live in Oregon. It was there, when I was forty years old, that I was a witness to another bizarre and mysterious event that baffled the world. Little did I know when I got on a plane in Portland that I'd be part of an unsolved crime.

It was the day before Thanksgiving in 1971 and I was flying to a family gathering in Seattle. It was no more than an hour's flight and not long after take-off, I noticed a man in the seat in front give the flight attendant a note. I wondered if he couldn't speak or couldn't communicate in English but when I saw the look on the attendant's face on reading that note, I knew something scary was kicking off. It was when he opened his briefcase to show wires, a battery and red sticks inside that some of us saw he had a bomb. You can imagine the panic from people sitting close by. We didn't know it then, but he was demanding parachutes and $200,000 in $20 bills.

I must have been asked to describe that man so many times. All I can say was that he was just a normal-looking guy – not much older than me, I guess. He wore a suit and a tie, had dark glasses and medium-length brownish hair. That's it – that's all there was to him. Apparently, he had signed in at the airport as D. B. Cooper, but that was just a made-up name.

Thankfully, the plane landed smoothly and the stewards ushered us all off in a hurry, while that man remained seated. It was only later that we read the story and realised that we were witnesses to one of the most mysterious robberies ever.

Once all the passengers were off that plane, the man hijacked it. As soon as he got his money and parachutes, he forced two pilots, a flight engineer and a flight attendant to stay on the plane. He ordered them to take off and fly to Mexico City. In the safety of the airport lounge, I watched that plane take off and disappear into the clouds. According to reports, the man tied all the bank notes to his body and strapped on a parachute. Shortly into the flight, he opened the plane door, lowered the rear steps and jumped from almost three kilometres high. They say the windchill up there would be minus 57 Celsius – enough to kill you in normal clothes. But the thing is, both the man and the money disappeared. The guy known as Mr Cooper from Flight 305 was never seen again.

I've often wondered about that man. Was he a trained parachutist or just a crank? Did he survive and live to spend all that money, or did he fall to his death? After all, he would have fallen into heavily wooded and rugged country. Of course, there were massive searches and years of dead-end leads. Then, in 1980, a boy found a decaying package containing $5,800 buried along the Columbia River. The serial numbers on those $20 bills matched those of the ransom money. Yet, after even more searches, nothing more was ever discovered. The FBI kept the case open for forty-five years until they finally closed it as UNSOLVED in 2016. That mystery of the man known only as 'D.B. Cooper' – who I saw – remains one of the eeriest unsolved crimes in American history. I guess it may never be solved. But like I always say, never say never.

Living in Oregon and at one time enjoying hiking out there in the great outdoors, I was bound to come across folks who'd met Sasquatch. That's Bigfoot to most Americans – the mythical ape-man we're often told doesn't exist.

Around a third of all Bigfoot sightings are reported in the state of Oregon, so that's thousands. I'm now one of the people who's spotted it, even though we're often told it doesn't exist.

It must be about twenty years ago now, when

my husband and I were spending a weekend in the wilderness – a remote hilly area with miles of thick forest. Our log cabin was by a lake, which we wanted for a peaceful time of fishing and boating. With the Blue Mountains nearby, we hoped to see a few eagles or elk but I was reassured wolves, bears and cougars would leave us alone. This was wild country but I didn't think for a moment that Bigfoot would show up at our camp.

Our cabin had a log burner, so when I awoke early one morning just as it was getting light, I thought I'd make myself useful by going outside to gather some wood. As I bent down to fill a large basket with branches, I saw a family of wild hogs foraging in the undergrowth. There was one adult and about six hoglets almost half-grown. Suddenly, out of nowhere, a huge hairy creature on two legs crashed through the trees. At first I thought it was a black bear and feared it was coming to attack me, but I soon realised it wasn't a bear at all. I would describe it as about three metres tall, covered in dark hair and with an unpleasant, ape-like face. It moved with plodding, ungainly strides and stumbled in the mud of the creek. By now the hogs were squealing and running off, but that creature lumbered after them, reached out with a long arm and grabbed one of the hogs. Making loud whooping noises, the creature stared at me, before growling and suddenly turning to shamble off up a slope into the forest. The poor hog gave a last bloodcurdling screech before everything went deathly quiet. I couldn't believe what I'd just seen and I made my way over to where the Sasquatch had appeared – for that's what I was sure it must have been. I was struck by two things: the enormous footprints in the mud and a strong, lingering unpleasant smell, like nothing I've ever known.

Although I was completely startled, I didn't panic as the Sasquatch didn't seem to be a threat to me. I went back indoors with my basket of wood and said, 'Honey, you'll never guess – I've just met a Bigfoot. Either that or a hefty man in a scary gorilla suit!'

I later reported what I had seen and a bunch of people came in a truck to investigate. They took plaster casts from those footprints, but they never caught sight of the creature. All the same, that night I slept with a heavy wooden club by my pillow – just in case.

When my great-grandma finished speaking into the microphone, she gave me a quick wink. 'It's been an interesting life,' she said with a wicked smile, 'and I can't wait for the next big surprise!'

MYSTERY FACTS

Did you know...

1. During an attempt to fly around the world in 1937, American aviator Amelia Earhart disappeared somewhere over the Pacific Ocean. The wreckage of her aircraft was never found, and her disappearance remains one of the big unsolved mysteries of the 20th century. Before her disappearance, Amelia Earhart was the first woman to fly solo across the Atlantic Ocean.

2. The search to find the Yeti can be traced back to the time of Alexander the Great, who in 326 BC set out to conquer the Indus Valley and demanded to see a Yeti for himself. Local people were unable to help. The name 'Abominable

SHIVERS

Snowman' wasn't used until the 1920s. In the 1950s the Nepali government cashed in on Yeti myths by issuing Yeti-hunting licences priced at £400 per Yeti. So far no one has succeeded in capturing a Yeti, dead or alive.

3. Mystery ape-men are reported from every continent except Antarctica. They include the Sasquatch of North America, the Yowie in Australia, the Yeren of China, the Almas of Russia and the Mapinguari of Brazil.

4. Belief in guardian angels can be traced throughout history, in many cultures. Surveys in the USA show that over half of all adults believe that they have been protected by a guardian angel during their life. In 2007, a poll suggested 68% of Americans believe that 'angels and demons are active in the world' and 20% said they had had an encounter with an angel or a devil. Surveys in Britain suggest about a third of people believe they have a guardian angel, while one in 10 people claim they have had contact with one. A poll showed that 39% of women and 26% of men believe in guardian angels.

5. Alien Big Cats (ABCs) are animals such as panthers and leopards which have been reported in areas far from their natural habitats. Sightings, tracks and remains of prey have been reported in countries such as Britain and across Europe, Canada, Australia, New Zealand and the USA. In British folklore, the Beast of Bodmin Moor is a wild panther-like cat living in the remote moorland of Cornwall. Sightings of ABCs are often reported in rural areas, as well as in suburbs outside some towns.

6. The Loch Ness Monster has long been of interest to scientists. In 1987 Operation Deepscan was the largest scientific search for 'Nessie' so far. After three days of scouring the deep waters with the latest sonar equipment, the biggest search for the monster ended with still more questions. A fleet of 24 boats spread out over Loch Ness to measure underwater signals. At one part of the lake, the sonar apparatus detected three large objects at depths of between 100–200 metres. A researcher said these could be living creatures 'larger than a shark but smaller than a whale'. However, boats failed to pick up any more traces when they returned to the same part of the loch on following days. The mystery lives on!

7. Perhaps the *Mary Celeste* sailing ship was always jinxed? Originally named *Amazon*, she was given a new name after a series of

mishaps, including the sudden illness and death of her first captain and a collision with another ship in the English Channel. After she was famously found deserted, an investigation into whether the *Dei Gratia*'s crew had 'stolen' her for salvage money found no evidence of foul play. Even so, many rumours spread, with *Mary Celeste* sailing under different owners for 12 years before her last captain deliberately ran her aground in Haiti as an attempted insurance fraud. All her dark secrets sank with her.

8. Both the story of Miracle Mike, the Wonder Chicken and that of D. B. Cooper jumping from a passenger plane really did happen. Miracle Mike has websites that celebrate this 'fowl mystery'. For many years after the disappearance of D. B. Cooper on 24th November 1971, the FBI investigated this case that baffled America. Just what really

happened to the mystery man who hijacked a Boeing 747 plane, then jumped out of the plane with the loot, never to be heard from again? We will probably never know.

9. Bigfoot legends go back at least 3,000 years, and a Cherokee legend tells of such a mysterious creature with the power to read people's minds. Ever since, Bigfoot sightings have been reported in every US state except Hawaii. According to a 2007 survey, only 16% of Americans said that Bigfoot 'absolutely' or 'probably' exists. 44% responded 'probably not' and another 40% insisted it 'absolutely does not' exist. Interestingly, nearly half of Americans in another survey (45%) believe in ghosts, demons and aliens.

10. The most famous Bigfoot sighting is the creature filmed by Roger Patterson and Bob

SHIVERS

Gimlin in the Bluff Creek region of northern California. Despite much investigation since that footage from 1967, it is still uncertain whether this was a hoax or a genuine sighting. Take a look at it online and decide for yourself – if you dare!

GLOSSARY

Bermuda Triangle an area in the Atlantic Ocean between Bermuda, Puerto Rico and Florida where ships and planes have apparently disappeared mysteriously.

Chupacabra a creature of legend said to live in parts of the Americas, with the first sightings reported in Puerto Rico. The name comes from its reputation for drinking the blood of goats.

Cryptozoology the study of creatures, such as the Chupacabra, the existence of which has not been scientifically proved.

Dire wolf an extinct wolf that was widespread in North America up to about 12,000 years ago, having a larger body and a smaller brain than today's wolf.

GLOSSARY

Ghost ship a ship with no living crew aboard; either a haunted vessel of folklore or a real derelict ship found adrift with its crew missing.

Guardian angel a spirit or being that is believed by some to protect and guide a particular person.

Inexplicable impossible to explain.

Jack the Ripper an unidentified murderer of great mystery who killed at least five women in London's East End in 1888.

Jersey Devil a legendary creature said to inhabit Southern New Jersey, USA – with the head of a goat, leathery bat-like wings, horns, small arms with clawed hands, cloven hooves, a forked tail and a 'blood-curdling scream'.

GLOSSARY

Spontaneous combustion the burning of a living body without an apparent external source of heat.

UFO any 'unidentified flying object' seen in the sky or landing on Earth, sometimes believed to be from another planet.

Yeti an ape-like creature taller than an average human, similar to the legendary Bigfoot, and said to live in parts of the Himalayas.